Lost in
the Storm!

For a long time the plane struggled through the wild tossing winds of the storm.

"Foster," Miss Pickerell said, "are we lost?"

Foster looked up. "We're still in the arctic," he said. "But it's impossible to know just how far we were driven by the storm, or in what direction. And unless the clouds open up so we can get a sight of the ground, we have no way of telling whether we are over land, open water or ice."

A shiver of fear ran through Miss Pickerell.

"Miss Pickerell!" Foster suddenly shouted. "We're running out of gasoline. There's only one thing to do. No matter what's under us, I'm going to have to try to make a crash landing."

D1264937

Miss Pickerell Goes to the Arctic

Ellen MacGregor

Illustrated by PAUL GALDONE

AN ARCHWAY PAPERBACK
POCKET BOOKS • NEW YORK

All of the characters in this book are fictitious.

 POCKET BOOKS, a Simon & Schuster division of
GULF & WESTERN CORPORATION
1230 Avenue of the Americas, New York, N.Y. 10020

Copyright 1954 by McGraw-Hill, Inc.

Published by arrangement with McGraw-Hill, Inc.
Library of Congress Catalog Card Number: 54-8816

ISBN: 0-671-56021-2

First Pocket Books printing February, 1981

10 9 8 7 6 5 4 3 2 1

AN ARCHWAY PAPERBACK and ARCH are trademarks
of Simon & Schuster.

Printed in the U.S.A.

IL 4+

To the Tacoma
and the Kent MacGregors

Contents

1

Miss Pickerell and Mr. Esticott

The man behind the soda fountain in the Square Toe City Drugstore, wearing a rather tight white jacket, stood reading a large red book that was propped up in front of him.

The man's name was Mr. Esticott.

Mr. Esticott's white jacket did not quite meet across his stomach, and it revealed that he was wearing a dark blue vest with gold buttons down the front of it. Mr. Esticott was the conductor on the train that ran between Square Toe City and the state capital. He only worked at the drugstore soda fountain between trains. It was just a part-time job.

The door of the drugstore opened, and Mr. Esticott looked up. "Hello, Miss Pickerell," he said.

Miss Pickerell stood sidewise in the opening, holding the door ajar with her foot while she briskly snapped her black umbrella open and shut several times to shake off all the rain.

Then she came inside, bought a newspaper from the druggist, crossed over to the soda fountain, and asked Mr. Esticott to make her an ice cream soda.

"Fortunately," said Mr. Esticott, laying aside his book, "I made up a fresh batch of peppermint syrup just yesterday, Miss Pickerell. I thought you might be coming in."

Peppermint was Miss Pickerell's favorite flavor. She always ordered a peppermint ice cream soda whenever she came to the Square Toe City Drugstore.

"I'd feel a little selfish being in here eating an ice cream soda while my cow is waiting outside," Miss Pickerell said, "except that I know she won't get wet. I've had a canvas awning made for her trailer, to keep her dry when it rains." Miss Pickerell took a paper napkin and wiped the rain off her glasses.

"That's a very becoming black hat you are wearing," said Mr. Esticott. "It goes well with your pink sweater. Your niece and nephew are well?"

"As far as I know they're well," said Miss Pickerell.

"I mean your oldest niece and your oldest nephew. The ones who are spending the summer with you to keep you company."

"For all the company Dwight and Rosemary are," said Miss Pickerell, "they might just as well be in the middle of the Arctic Ocean. Dwight and Rosemary are licensed amateur radio operators and they spend all their time at their short-wave radio set talking to people they've never even seen. Everytime *I* start to say anything to them, they tell me to 'Sh!' "

Mr. Esticott put Miss Pickerell's ice cream soda on the counter in front of her, and she put a straw in it and tasted it. It was delicious.

Holding the ice cream soda in one hand, Miss Pickerell walked over to the store window and looked out to make sure that her cow, outside in the little canvas-covered trailer, was all right. Miss Pickerell and her cow were very good friends, and whenever Miss Pickerell had errands to do in Square Toe City the cow accompanied her.

The cow seemed to be comfortable, and Miss Pickerell returned to her stool at the soda fountain. She pointed to the large red book Mr. Esticott had been reading.

"I'm glad to see you've finally finished reading my encyclopedia," she said.

Mr. Esticott cleared his throat. "I haven't exactly finished it, Miss Pickerell. Not quite. But this is the last volume. This is the W-X-Y-Z volume, and I'm sure that if I take it with me every day to read on the train when I'm not busy collecting tickets that I'll have it finished in another week or two, so that—"

"Now see here, Mr. Esticott!" Miss Pickerell said. "The only reason I agreed to let you read my encyclopedia was that you promised to have it finished long before this. Don't you remember that day you asked me if I'd let you take it to read on the train when you weren't busy collecting tickets? You assured me at the time that you are a very fast reader."

"I *am* a very fast reader, Miss Pickerell. It's just that your encyclopedia is so inter-

"You've finally finished reading my encyclopedia"

esting that I've been distracted by some of the things I've read about."

"I'm afraid I shall have to insist on your giving it back to me anyway," Miss Pickerell said. "I keep thinking of things. You know how it is when you think of something like that. You want to look it up right away."

"The H volume was very interesting," said Mr. Esticott.

"If Dwight and Rosemary didn't spend all their time at their short-wave radio set," Miss Pickerell said, "if they had a little time to talk to me once in a while, I wouldn't keep thinking of things to look up."

"On the whole though," said Mr. Esticott, "the H volume wasn't so interesting as some of the others. Take the B volume for instance. There are a great many interesting things in that volume. You can have your niece and nephew read that volume first. By then I'll probably be through with this—"

"I don't want it for my niece and nephew," Miss Pickerell said. "I want it for myself. And I don't want to read it. I just want to be able to look things up when—"

"Next to the B volume," said Mr. Esticott, "the S volume is probably the most interesting. In fact, if those two books hadn't been so full of information, I would have finished reading the whole set a lot sooner. But I got so interested in the article on bird banding that I began to study about how it's possible to tell what parts of the world birds migrate to by putting lightweight identification bands around their legs and then releasing them. Where the birds are found shows how far away they have migrated."

"That *is* interesting," Miss Pickerell agreed.

"There's one kind of bird—" said Mr. Esticott, "it's called the arctic tern—that flies practically all the way from the South Pole to the North Pole every spring. In the summer, arctic terns make their nests and hatch their baby birds all over the arctic regions. Then, when it starts to be winter, they fly all the way to the other side of the world—to the antarctic regions."

"That doesn't seem very sensible," Miss Pickerell said. "Why don't they stop in some nice warm country to spend the winter?"

"A lot of birds do that," Mr. Esticott

7

said. "I don't know if you realize it, Miss Pickerell, but there are over 8,600 different species of birds in the world. And each species has its own special route of migration. Banding birds is a way to find out what parts of the world different kinds of birds migrate to."

Miss Pickerell was thoughtful. "I wish Dwight and Rosemary were interested in banding birds instead of being amateur radio operators," she said. "Then maybe I could say something to them once in a while without having them tell me to 'Sh!' "

"They couldn't be bird banders," Mr. Esticott said. "They couldn't be licensed bird banders until they were eighteen years old. And not even then—unless they were familiar enough with different kinds of birds so that they wouldn't make a mistake about what kind of bird it was they were banding. Then, right in that same volume, there's a very interesting article on bush pilots. You can see now, I think, why it has taken me so long to finish reading the whole set."

"I don't think that excuses you," Miss Pickerell said. "You *did* promise."

"I showed the article about bush pilots to my cousin," said Mr. Esticott. "My cousin is a retired bush pilot. His name is Foster."

"Don't bush pilots fly up around the North Pole?" Miss Pickerell asked.

"Somewhere up around there," Mr. Esticott said. "Bush pilots fly around the arctic regions in places where there isn't any regular airplane service. Bush pilots will fly almost anywhere that anyone wants them to go. How about another ice cream soda, Miss Pickerell?"

Miss Pickerell shook her head and reached out for the encyclopedia volume.

So did Mr. Esticott. "I tell you what, Miss Pickerell," he said. "Why don't they call me up on the telephone? Your niece and nephew I mean. If they want to look up anything in the W-X-Y-Z volume, they can just call me here at the drugstore and let meread it to them. That is, if I'm not on the train collecting tickets, they can."

"I'm afraid the arrangement wouldn't be very satisfactory," Miss Pickerell said. "And anyway, *I'm* the one who wants the ency—"

"Suppose they wanted to look up something about the weather," said Mr. Esticott. "Or possibly you yourself. Don't hesitate to call me."

"When I want to know something about the weather," Miss Pickerell said, "I go to the weather station to find out."

She got down off the stool and picked up her umbrella.

"In fact, that's just where I'm going right now. I have to find out if there is going to be another blizzard next winter, like the one we had last year."

"Blizzard!" Mr. Esticott said. "Why, it's the middle of summer."

"I know," Miss Pickerell said. "And it's none too soon to be making plans. If there is the slightest danger of such a thing again this year, I shall take my cow to some warm part of the country. I wouldn't dream of asking her to go through such an experience again."

From outside, they heard the long drawn-out whistle of a train.

"Oh, excuse me, Miss Pickerell," Mr. Esticott said. He quickly took off his white jacket and hung it on a nail. Then he reached around behind a showcase and produced his blue conductor's coat and his conductor's hat. "That's the engineer signaling me. He always gives me plenty of warning so I won't miss the train. You

10

don't mind, do you, if I take this book along to read when I'm not busy collecting tickets?''

He had put on his coat and was picking up the encyclopedia volume. Miss Pickerell noticed that the druggist was coming across the store to take care of the soda fountain.

''I suppose not,'' Miss Pickerell said. ''But I do wish you'd try to be finished with it by the day after tomorrow. You could give it to me on the train. I'm going to the state capital on the train day after tomorrow to buy a birthday present for my cow.'' She followed the conductor to the door.

''Oh, Miss Pickerell!'' the druggist called out. ''Here's your newspaper. You almost forgot it.''

Mr. Esticott held the door open for Miss Pickerell while she put up her umbrella. Then he slid the book under his coat to keep it dry and sprinted down the street to the railroad station.

Miss Pickerell tucked the newspaper under her arm and rejoined her cow, who had been patiently waiting all this time under the canvas awning of her little red trailer.

2

A Surprise for Miss Pickerell's Cow

Miss Pickerell was disappointed to learn that the man in the weather station couldn't tell her whether or not there would be a blizzard next winter.

"I'm surprised to hear you say that," Miss Pickerell said, as she sat down in the chair he had offered her. "It was my understanding that the Weather Bureau is getting very good at making long-range forecasts."

"We aren't *that* good, Miss Pickerell," the man said. "At least not yet. All the time we are working to improve our knowledge, but the best we can do right now is to make thirty-day forecasts. If that would help you any—" He began to shuffle through some charts and papers on his desk. Then he looked up. "Or," he said. "a five-day forecast. Would you care to know what we are predicting in the way of weather for five days from now?"

"I certainly would," Miss Pickerell said. "If the weather is going to be sunny. It's on account of a surprise I'm planning."

"A surprise?"

"A birthday surprise," Miss Pickerell said. "For my cow. Every year, just before my cow's birthday, I take a pail, paint it some bright color, fill it with earth, and plant seeds of my cow's very favorite kind of grass. I always plant it early enough so that the grass in the pail will be well grown by the time of her birthday."

"What a quaint custom," said the man.

"It isn't any more quaint, is it," said Miss Pickerell, "than making a cake for the birthday of someone you like very much?"

"I suppose not," said the man. "You let her eat it?"

"Of course," said Miss Pickerell. "I've done this for my cow's birthday every year since she was one year old. I've done it so often I don't suppose she is really surprised any more. By this time it's more a tradition than a surprise. But I certainly would hate to have anything go wrong. I wouldn't want to disappoint her."

"With all the rain we've been having," the man said, "you must have quite a lush crop of grass growing in the pail."

"That's just the trouble," Miss Pickerell said. "The grass is tall and thick, but the flowers, on account of not having any sun the last few days, still aren't—"

"Flowers!"

"Why, yes," Miss Pickerell said. "I always plant a few bright-colored flowers in the pail too. I plant them so that they will be all in bloom by the time of the birthday. But this year, because there's been so little sun lately—"

"I know," the man said. "I'm afraid we'll find a good many flowers will be late this season. It's a good thing your flowers aren't really important. It's grass that matters to a cow. Your cow probably won't even notice about the flowers."

"Listen!" Miss Pickerell said. "If somebody made *you* a birthday cake, and then didn't take the trouble to put any frosting or any candles on it to make it pretty, *you'd* notice it, wouldn't you?"

14

"Well, I suppose so," said the man. "Since you put it that way. I don't wonder you're discouraged."

"If it weren't so impractical," said Miss Pickerell, "I'd just take the whole pail somewhere where it would get lots of sun."

"You'd take it south?"

"No," Miss Pickerell said. "North."

"But Miss Pickerell!"

"It's true, isn't it," Miss Pickerell said, "that the sun shines twenty-four hours a day at the North Pole in the summer time?"

"Well, yes," the man said. "But—"

"If I just knew someone who was going—" Miss Pickerell said. "But it would have to be somebody who could bring the pail back again by Friday. Friday is my cow's birthday."

Miss Pickerell knew that it would be perfectly possible for someone to fly to the north polar regions and get back again by Friday. She knew that the shortest way to fly from certain cities in our country to certain cities in Europe or Asia is to fly right over the top of the world—right over the north polar regions. She had measured it on a globe and knew it was true.

The man picked up a sheet of paper from his desk and looked at it with a slight frown.

"According to this advisory I have in my hand," he said, "weather conditions in the north polar regions don't look very good for the next few days."

"Well, I'm not going anyway," said Miss Pickerell. "It was just a thought."

"If the weather deteriorates," the man continued, "—that's what we say when we mean the weather is going to get worse— your plane might not be able to get through. And according to the information in this advisory, the weather up there *is* going to deteriorate in the next few days."

"I don't quite understand," Miss Pickerell said, "how you know so much about what's going to happen to the weather at the North Pole, when you can't even tell me if we're going to have a blizzard right here at home."

"It's because there are weather stations in different parts of the arctic regions," the man said, "that are continually taking weather measurements and readings. It's very important work because the kind of weather we have down here depends partly on what the weather is like at the North

Pole. When cold air from up there starts moving down toward us and collides with warm air coming up from the equator, it can cause a storm.''

Miss Pickerell went right on.

''After all my farm is only twenty-seven miles outside Square Toe City,'' she said. ''You can't tell me if there is going to be a blizzard just twenty-seven miles away. Yet you presume to know that there is going to be a storm at the North Pole.''

''I don't 'presume' any such thing,'' the man said. ''There is a *possibility* of stormy weather in the arctic regions. I can only advise you of the facts. As to the likelihood of a blizzard here next winter, my advice to you is to come to see us next fall and ask for a thirty-day forecast. We might be able to warn you a month ahead of time if there is going to be a blizzard. But certainly not now. Certainly not six months ahead of time.''

Miss Pickerell thanked him and tried to be polite about it, although his information had been most unsatisfactory. She realized that there were many factors to be taken into consideration in making weather forecasts, and that it was not an easy job.

She stood up to leave.

17

"I wouldn't worry about your flowers," the man said. "Even if it rains every minute until Friday."

Miss Pickerell looked at him, puzzled.

"Scientists have discovered," the man said, "that you can make many plants grow faster and better by keeping them in artificial light. That way they get light even after the sun goes down. If you just had some room in your home where you could leave the lights on almost all the time—"

Miss Pickerell remembered the room where Dwight and Rosemary had their short-wave radio set and how they sat up listening almost half the night. "I'm certainly very grateful to you for the suggestion."

It wasn't until after supper that night that Miss Pickerell had a chance to sit down in her kitchen rocking chair and read her newspaper.

It was Rosemary's turn to wash the dishes, so right after eating, Dwight had gone back to the short-wave radio set in the next room.

The newspaper told about an expedition that was being sent to the arctic regions to make a type of weather observation based on a study of glaciers.

18

Miss Pickerell had never heard of anything like this before, and it was so interesting that she started to read the article out loud to Rosemary.

She had just begun the first sentence when there was a knock at her kitchen door.

3

Foster, the Retired Bush Pilot

Rosemary reached out to the back door, which was right beside the sink, and opened it.

A young man was standing there.

He was a tall, well-built young man, wearing a leather jacket. He had rumpled brown hair, and his complexion was ruddy, as though he spent a great deal of time out of doors. And he was holding a whole pile of encyclopedia volumes balanced on his arm.

"I'm returning these for my cousin," he said, as Miss Pickerell got up and came toward the door. "My cousin is Mr. Esticott."

Miss Pickerell asked him to put the books on the kitchen table. She remembered now that Mr. Esticott had said that he had a cousin who was a retired bush pilot. But she couldn't quite remember the bush pilot's name. "You must be—?" she said.

"Foster," said the young man. "Foster Esticott."

Miss Pickerell introduced him to Rosemary and asked him to sit down.

"I wish I could," Foster said, and Miss Pickerell noticed how his eyes were shining. He seemed to be experiencing some happy sort of excitement. "But something pretty wonderful has happened. At least I hope it's going to happen. I wonder if you noticed an article in that paper you were reading about a weather expedition that is going to the arctic regions?"

"Yes." Miss Pickerell and Rosemary both said "Yes" at the same time, and they stopped and smiled at each other.

"I used to be a bush pilot," Foster said. "And I've never been really happy since I gave it up. The wonderful thing about this expedition is that they are planning to make their observations in the very part of the arctic that I'm most familiar with. I've

"I used to be a bush pilot"

been a bush pilot all over that part of the polar regions. I'm sure I could persuade them to let me be their pilot if I could just talk to them. I know that one of the men in the expedition has a short-wave radio in his home. And when my cousin got home from the train tonight and told me about how you"—he turned to Rosemary—"and your brother have a short-wave station, I thought maybe you'd let me—"

"Why, of course," Rosemary said.

And Miss Pickerell said, "The dishes can wait. Or maybe I'll do them later."

They all went into the next room where Dwight had someone in conversation. He signed off when Rosemary explained who Foster was and what he wanted. Dwight stood up and shook hands with Foster. Then the three of them sat down in front of the set, while Miss Pickerell brought her rocking chair in and sat down in a corner of the room, beside the pail of grass that she had put there that afternoon under a light bulb.

Miss Pickerell couldn't help feeling a little left out of things. But at least it was fun to listen.

Dwight contacted the expedition member's short-wave set, and then gave Foster the earphones.

It was apparent at once, from Foster's conversation, that the expedition wanted him to be their pilot. The only difficulty seemed to be that Foster might not be able to get his plane ready in time.

"Yes," he said. "Yes, I brought my plane with me when I came outside." Miss Pickerell knew that many people in the far north said they were going "outside" when they meant they were leaving the arctic. When they went back to the arctic, they said they were going "inside."

"Yes," Foster said again. "I'll get right to work on her. I'll get her in shape for the flight just as fast as I possibly can. Over."

He flipped a switch and listened intently for several minutes. Then he flipped the switch again. "I understand," he said. "You might have to leave with someone else if I'm not ready. Well, that's a chance I'll have to take." Then he said a few words of good-by.

Almost immediately after thanking Dwight and Rosemary and explaining to Miss Pickerell that Mr. Esticott hoped to have the last volume of the encyclopedia finished by the time she got on the train the day after tomorrow, Foster left. He mustn't lose a minute, he said, in getting his plane in shape for the flight. If he could only be ready in time, it would give him a chance to return to the arctic area which he knew and loved so well.

Miss Pickerell, although she couldn't imagine anybody loving the arctic, hoped with all her heart that he would succeed.

4

Model X24

Two days later, on the train going to the state capital, Miss Pickerell still hadn't made up her mind what to get for her cow's birthday. She had to decide on something by the time the train arrived because the only reason she was making the trip was to get her cow a present.

Miss Pickerell always liked to take a little snack along with her when she was traveling. She had just opened her box of lunch, and had just spread a white linen napkin on the red plush seat beside her, when the train entered a tunnel.

When the train came out of the tunnel, Miss Pickerell was embarrassed to find that she was staring straight into the dark brown eyes of the man sitting opposite her.

He had boarded the train an hour ago at the last stop.

"Would you care for a piece of fried chicken?" she asked, holding out a drumstick wrapped in waxed paper.

The man shook his head, lowered his gaze, and then resumed the position he had occupied for the past hour—staring glumly out of the window, his arm on the window sill and his chin supported by the palm of his hand.

Mr. Esticott came down the aisle with the last volume of the encyclopedia under his arm.

"How about you, Mr. Esticott?" Miss Pickerell asked, as he stopped beside her seat.

"Thank you, Miss Pickerell," the conductor said. "I don't mind if I do." He sat down in the empty seat beside the man in the brown suit, who was still staring out of the window. "Your cow is well?"

Miss Pickerell handed him the drumstick.

"My cow is well now," she said. "But I worry about her when I think of next winter. If I could just *know* whether there is going to be a blizzard, then I could make some plans for her. I could arrange—"

Miss Pickerell stopped because at the word "blizzard" the man in the brown suit had suddenly come to life. He turned away from the window and looked directly at Miss Pickerell with his deep brown eyes.

"Allow me," he said, removing his wallet from an inside pocket of his coat, "to introduce myself."

He took a card from his wallet, stood up, and handed the card to Miss Pickerell.

The card read:

MOBILE HOMES

Bellingham Busby
Sales Engineer

"Are you sure you won't change your mind about the fried chicken, Mr. Busby?" Miss Pickerell asked when she had read the card. "There's plenty more here in my box. Or perhaps a piece of solid chocolate layer cake."

"No, no," Mr. Busby said impatiently. "I'm too unhappy to eat." He gave another of his cards to Mr. Esticott who promptly stuck it into the encyclopedia for a bookmark. Mr. Busby sat down again.

"Excuse me," said Mr. Esticott. "I have to go and announce the next stop."

Miss Pickerell looked again at the card in her hand. Just what are 'mobile homes'?" she asked.

Mr. Busby crossed his legs and leaned back in his seat. "Mobile homes," he said, "is the modern-day term for what used to be called trailers. Our factory is in the state capital and I'm—"

"Oh, I know all about trailers," Miss Pickerell said. "I have one myself. It's a little red wooden trailer with a piece of canvas over the top of it to keep—"

"From what you say," said Mr. Busby, "I would gather that there is practically no resemblance at all between your trailer and the trailers that my company manufactures. The trailers manufactured by Mobile Homes are to *live* in. In any part of the world. Under any conditions. We even make trailers to order, if a person has special requirements. I'm the company's sales—"

"I notice here on your card," Miss Pickerell said, "that you are a sales engineer.

"I have to go and announce the next stop"

I suppose that means that you are partly a salesman and partly an engineer?''

"I prefer," said Mr. Busby rather stiffly, "to think of myself as *both* a salesman and an engineer. In the modern-day world it is not enough for a salesman to be able to sell things. He also has to be able to operate them. Put me down in any part of the world—any part at all—with one of our mobile homes, even if it was specially manufactured, and I'd be able to operate it. That's what it means to be a sales engineer. That's why I was capable of demonstrating our new model snowmobile to an expedition that's going to the arctic regions to study weather conditions."

Miss Pickerell remembered about Foster's conversation on Dwight and Rosemary's short-wave radio the night before last. This was probably the same expedition that Foster wanted to use his plane for.

"I was supposed to go with them," Mr. Busby said, "and take Model X24 along."

"Model X24?"

"It's our very latest model snowmobile. A snowmobile is sort of a combination trailer and tractor built and equipped in such a way that people can travel in it quite comfortably in all sorts of winter conditions. Model X24 is a three-axle vehicle with two skis in front instead of front wheels. The two back wheels on each side have a revolving tread that runs around both of them; so it is just as if the snowmobile carried its own road along with it."

Miss Pickerell was trying to picture what a snowmobile looked like from Mr. Busby's description, but she wasn't quite sure she understood.

"But they couldn't wait for me," Mr. Busby said sadly. "I didn't even get a chance to *tell* them about the advantages of Model X24. I had an appointment to see them at ten o'clock this morning, but they had to leave very early in the morning because they were afraid the weather was going to deteriorate if they waited any longer."

Miss Pickerell hoped that Foster had been able to get his plane ready in time to take the expedition to the arctic.

"What *are* some of the advantages of Model X24?" Miss Pickerell wanted to know.

"For one thing," Mr. Busby said, "it's big enough so that they could put their weather instruments into it and drive over the ice and snow to wherever they wanted to make observations. There's a short-wave radio in it too, and a heater that runs on batteries so that even if they got caught in an arctic storm, they could still be snug and warm.''

An idea was forming in the back of Miss Pickerell's mind.

"I feel very badly about it," Mr. Busby said. "I don't know anybody else to try to sell Model X24 to—except possibly one person I've heard about."

"Mr. Busby!" Miss Pickerell sat straight up and looked right at Mr. Busby. "You've just given me a wonderful idea. I wonder if your snowmobile could be adapted so that a cow could be comfortable in it."

"It's strange that you should ask that," said Mr. Busby. "On account of this person I just mentioned. I understand that there is a person who lives on a farm near Square Toe City who has a cow she is very fond of. And it's just possible that she might—"

"That person is—"

"Not you!" Mr. Busby looked surprised. "Are you sure?"

"Well, of course I'm sure," Miss Pickerell said. "Aren't you sure you're Mr. Busby?"

"I almost wish I weren't," Mr. Busby said. "Unless I can sell Model X24, it will spoil my sales record. According to my information this party with the cow—"

"Please don't call me a 'party,' " said Miss Pickerell. "My name is Miss Pickerell."

"According to my information, this person—this Miss Pickerell—is so devoted to her cow that she never goes anywhere unless the cow goes too."

"That," said Miss Pickerell, "was before my oldest niece and my oldest nephew came to spend the summer with me. They are very reliable, and my cow likes them, so I never have the slightest hesitation about leaving her in their care when it's necessary."

"I see," said Mr. Busby. He uncrossed his legs and leaned forward. "Now what you need, Miss Pickerell, for your pet that you are so fond of, is a trailer."

"My cow already has a trailer," Miss Pickerell said. "However, I've just been thinking—"

"Suppose we should have a severe winter again next year," Mr. Busby said. "Suppose there should be a blizzard!"

"I know," said Miss Pickerell. "I've been worrying about that myself."

"I guess if we had a blizzard next year," said Mr. Busby, "you'd be pretty glad if you had one of our snowmobiles for your cow. It could easily be adapted for her use. Take our Model X24—"

"What does the 'X' stand for?" asked Miss Pickerell.

" 'X' means 'experimental,' " said Mr. Busby. " 'X' is always used on the number of a model that is still being tested."

"Then I wouldn't be interested," said Miss Pickerell. "Not at all. I wouldn't care to ask my cow to ride in a vehicle that was experimental. Something might happen."

"You don't understand," said Mr. Busby. "Model X24 has been thoroughly tested to stand up under any winter conditions we are likely to have in this part of the world. All the 'X' means is that it hasn't been completely tested for *arctic* conditions."

"Could it be delivered by Friday?" Miss Pickerell asked.

"Unless you'd like to have it stored for you at the factory," said Mr. Busby. "Until next winter. It's all ready to be sent to the arctic. There's even a cargo parachute attached to the pallet. A pallet is a strong, lightweight platform that things are put on to make them easier to handle when they are being shipped or moved or dropped from a plane."

Miss Pickerell clapped her hands together. "Drop it by parachute in the middle of my cow's pasture," she said. "That way it will be a real birthday surprise for her."

Mr. Busby scratched his chin. "I'll see what I can do," he said. "And now that I've sold the snowmobile, and won't have to spoil my sales record, my appetite seems to have improved. Perhaps. . . . If you still have some left, I might eat a bit of fried chicken."

"Yes, of course," said Miss Pickerell, passing him a piece.

When Mr. Esticott came down the aisle to get some cake, Miss Pickerell told him what had happened.

"I can just hardly wait for Friday," she said. "I think Friday is going to be the very nicest birthday my cow has ever had."

36

It would have surprised Miss Pickerell very much if she had known what was going to happen—if she had known that by the time Friday arrived, she would be far, far away from Square Toe City and her cow.

5

Disaster in the Arctic

When Miss Pickerell returned to Square
Toe City, Dwight was waiting for her at
the railroad station. He had promised to
drive Miss Pickerell's car and meet the
train.

On the way home, Miss Pickerell told
Dwight about the snowmobile she had
bought for her cow's birthday present, and
Dwight commented on how well her pail
of flowers was developing, now that she
had put it inside the house, right under a
light bulb that was on most of the time.

Rosemary had supper all ready for them
when they arrived.

It wasn't until Tuesday that Miss Pickerell found out that Foster hadn't been able

to get his plane ready in time to take the weather expedition to the far north. He came out to Miss Pickerell's farm Tuesday night to return the last volume of her encyclopedia which Mr. Esticott had finally finished.

Foster seemed so unhappy and disappointed that Miss Pickerell didn't question him. All he said was that the expedition had to leave before he had his plane quite ready. They had had to take a different plane, piloted by another pilot. Then he quickly changed the subject, as if the disappointment was too painful to think about any more.

"There's only one good thing about it," he said. "Now that I've got my plane in shape again, several people have wanted to hire my services." And he told Miss Pickerell that he had been engaged by Mr. Busby to drop the snowmobile in her cow's pasture on Friday.

"I've had a lot of experience dropping cargoes," he said. "When I was a bush pilot."

On Wednesday came the news that shocked the whole world.

The weather expedition plane was lost!

Somewhere in the vast reaches of the arctic the weather plane was down. Whether it had landed safely, whether there were any survivors, no one knew.

An arctic air base had picked up a radio message from the plane an hour after it had stopped there to refuel. It was a routine message. No trouble had been indicated. But from that moment on, there had been no word.

All over that part of the arctic rescue planes were searching, but the area to be covered was vast. When last heard from, the plane had had an almost full supply of gasoline. It might have come down almost immediately, or it might have gone on for hours until its fuel was exhausted. If there had been trouble, the pilot might have changed the course. The plane might have gone in any direction.

Like many other amateur radio operators, Dwight and Rosemary, between them, manned their short-wave radio station all night long. Although such a thing was much more likely to happen in the winter, they explained to Miss Pickerell that sometimes freakish atmospheric conditions made direct radio contact in the arctic impossible. And sometimes, during these conditions, a locally broadcast arctic radio message had been picked up long distances away.

But this time neither Dwight nor Rosemary nor any other radio operator anywhere in the world picked up any distress signal from the arctic. There was no word of the missing plane.

And all this time, Miss Pickerell kept wishing there was something she herself could do to help.

On Thursday morning Foster called Miss Pickerell from the Square Toe City airport. He asked her permission to drop the snowmobile in her cow's pasture right away instead of waiting until Friday.

"I must go," he said. "I know that part of the arctic well, and I want to go and take part in the search. The snowmobile is already loaded in my plane. As soon as I drop it, and as soon as I find someone to go along as an observer, I'm leaving for the north. I hope I'll be able to find an observer. It's always better if two people are looking."

Without a moment's hesitation, Miss Pickerell said, "I'll go. I'll be your observer."

"Can you be ready to leave right away?

As soon as I drop your snowmobile?"

"Wouldn't it be useful for rescue operations?" Miss Pickerell asked. "If we should find the missing plane?"

"It might," said Foster.

"Then I'll meet you at the airport just as soon as Dwight can drive me there," said Miss Pickerell.

She hated to ask Dwight to do it, especially since he had had so little sleep the night before, but when Miss Pickerell told them of her conversation with Foster, both he and Rosemary agreed instantly that she should go.

While Miss Pickerell was saying a hasty farewell to her cow, and trying to explain about why she wouldn't be there for the cow's birthday, Rosemary got together the things she thought Miss Pickerell would need in the arctic and rolled them up inside her own Girl Scout sleeping bag. Dwight put the pack in the back seat of the automobile.

At the very last minute Miss Pickerell decided to take her black umbrella. With the sun shining twenty-four hours a day at the North Pole, it might be convenient to have it for shade.

6

Miss Pickerell Goes to the Rescue

Miss Pickerell was surprised to find Mr. Busby waiting for her at the airport. As soon as Dwight stopped the car, Mr. Busby came hurrying toward them.

He seemed like a different person from the one Miss Pickerell had met on the train a few days ago. For the first time Miss Pickerell noticed his forceful-looking jaw. There was something about his voice when he spoke that made him seem like a person who was accustomed to being in authority. Also, he acted like a person who was used to making quick decisions.

"Now then," he said, after he and

Dwight had been introduced, "Foster's plane is right over there and here's exactly what we're going to do."

"No, we aren't," Miss Pickerell said, "if you're talking about dropping the snowmobile in my cow's pasture."

"Foster told me all about it," Mr. Busby said. "I admire your spirit, Miss Pickerell. We're almost ready to start."

"You're going too?"

"Have you forgotten," said Mr. Busby, "that I'm a sales *engineer?* When I sell a product I consider it part of my responsibility to see that the customer learns how to use it. Wherever the customer goes, I go too. I'm at home in any part of the world."

Foster came up to them. He took Miss Pickerell's pack from Dwight's hand. "Any time you are ready," he said. "Everything is in order and ready to go."

Miss Pickerell said good-by to Dwight and promised to send him and Rosemary a short-wave radio message if she got a chance. Then she and Foster and Mr. Busby walked to the plane.

"I hope you aren't expecting too much in the way of luxury, Miss Pickerell," Foster said. "My plane, as you can see, is designed more for utility than for comfort.''

Foster was certainly right about that. The inside was one large compartment, with the pilot's seat at the front where the windows were. The back was all enclosed, but Miss Pickerell could make out a huge tractorlike vehicle, almost as big as a trailer, lashed to a narrow metal platform. Miss Pickerell supposed this metal platform was the pallet Mr. Busby had mentioned.

"You and I will take these two seats in the middle," Mr. Busby said to her.

The seats had their backs to the outside walls of the plane, and were facing each other. Miss Pickerell had never ridden sideways in an airplane before. It was a novel sensation. Also it seemed strange not to be able to look out.

"In a cargo plane," Mr. Busby said, "the cargo comes first. Passenger seats have to be fitted in where they can."

Foster took his place and began to warm up the engines. They were noisy. And also, after the plane got into the air, the ride was a bit bumpy.

"Look!" Foster shouted a few moments later, and motioned to them to come forward.

"Forevermore!" Miss Pickerell said, as she looked down and recognized that they were flying right over her own farm. She saw her cow in one corner of the pasture and Rosemary waving to them from the back steps. It made her homesick for just a moment, until she reminded herself of the purpose of their trip—how they were hoping to be able to help in the rescue of the poor men who had been lost in the arctic.

When they were back at their seats, Mr. Busby said, "We aren't going to waste any time stopping until we have to stop to refuel, and that won't be for a long time yet because Foster had extra fuel tanks attached to our wings to increase our range."

"Won't Foster get sleepy, though?" Miss Pickerell asked.

"When he does," said Mr. Busby, "I'll take over the controls. In addition to being a sales engineer, I'm also a pilot."

Miss Pickerell leaned back in her seat and dozed off. She slept fitfully. She kept waking up. She had the feeling she had done something foolish. But each time, before she could quite figure out what it was, she went to sleep again.

Finally she came awake suddenly. She

*Miss Pickerell leaned back in her seat
and dozed*

knew what it was that had been worrying her.

"Mr. Busby," she said. "I've been terribly stupid. I offered to bring my snowmobile to the arctic. But it's summer. Even in the arctic it's summer and the sun will be shining twenty-four hours a day. What good will a snowmobile be—even if we do find the survivors—if there isn't any snow for it to run on?"

"There'll be plenty of snow," Mr. Busby said. "And ice too, because we're going so far north. It may be that the missing plane is down somewhere on the north polar ice pack—that's a huge mass of drifting ice, several million square miles large, that occupies the Arctic Ocean. Now you'd better try to go to sleep again, Miss Pickerell."

When Miss Pickerell awoke the next time, Mr. Busby had just poured some hot soup from a Thermos bottle. He offered it to Miss Pickerell, together with a package of sandwiches wrapped in waxed paper.

"You've been asleep a long time, Miss Pickerell," he said. "You must be hungry."

"How far have we come?" Miss Pickerell asked. The food tasted very good.

"You'll be surprised to learn, Miss Pickerell, that we've almost reached the Arctic Circle."

"Already!" Miss Pickerell couldn't believe it. "But Foster's still piloting," she said.

"Foster and I have changed places twice already," Mr. Busby said. "You slept right through."

When Miss Pickerell started to stand up to stretch her legs, she knew this must be true, because her whole body felt so stiff.

Foster shouted something to them over his shoulder.

"Come on!" Mr. Busby said. "We're just flying over the Arctic Circle."

"Oh, how exciting!" Miss Pickerell said. She knew, of course, that she couldn't see the Arctic Circle—that it is just a line on a map—but it was thrilling to know that she had actually reached the arctic regions.

Mr. Busby steadied her elbow as they went forward and looked out over Foster's shoulder.

"I don't know just what I expected," Miss Pickerell said, "but I didn't know the arctic looked like this."

Foster spoke up. "That's the tundra," he said.

49

"But it's so bare and flat, and sort of greenish-yellow," Miss Pickerell said. "And nothing growing. No trees."

"There's plenty growing," Foster said. "If we were down there, you'd see all kinds of beautiful flowers. And millions of birds. Insects too. Especially mosquitoes."

"Mosquitoes!" Miss Pickerell exclaimed. "In the arctic?"

"This time of year, for a few weeks," Foster said, "mosquitoes are worse in the arctic than they are anywhere in the world."

"Forevermore!" said Miss Pickerell. "There are an awful lot of little lakes, aren't there?"

"Yes," said Foster, "and the ground down there is pretty spongy and soft from all the melted snow. The melted snow water can't soak down through the ground because of the permafrost."

"Does permafrost mean what it sounds like?" Miss Pickerell asked. "Does it mean something that is permanently frozen?"

Foster said, "Yes. The ground in the arctic is permanently frozen. Every summer the top layer thaws out, although

50

sometimes at night it freezes over again. But farther down the soil *never* thaws out. It's that permanently frozen layer of the earth that's called the permafrost.''

Foster turned his head toward Mr. Busby.

"I think, Mr. Busby," he said, "that when we stop to refuel, we'd better change our landing wheels to the floats that we brought with us. Just to be on the safe side. If we *did* get forced down for any reason, we could land on one of the little lakes if we had floats. But the ground is too spongy for us to be able to land on wheels.''

"Just as you say, Foster," Mr. Busby said. "You're the bush pilot. You're the one who has had arctic experience.''

"There's a place about half an hour from here," Foster said, "where I arranged to have some fuel cached. That was last week when I thought I'd be piloting the weather expedition. It's the one place around here where the ground is fairly hard and level. I don't think I'll have any difficulty landing there with wheels. At least I never have before.''

Miss Pickerell became aware of something that had been bothering her. It seemed rude to mention it, but she thought she'd better.

"I'm afraid, Foster," she said, "that we're off our course. We aren't going north."

"Oh, yes we are," said Mr. Busby.

"No," Miss Pickerell said. She pointed to the sun, low in the sky ahead of them. "We're going west. We're going right straight toward the sunset."

"It seems so because we are so far north now, Miss Pickerell," Foster explained. "But it isn't sunset. It's almost midnight. From up here, the rotation of the earth makes it seem as though the sun is going all the way around the horizon. In the winter, of course, the sun goes all the way around *below* the horizon, and it stays dark for several months."

"Oh," said Miss Pickerell. She was trying to figure this out when Foster spoke again to Mr. Busby.

"Our next fueling stop," Foster said, "will be at an arctic air base. We'll find out there whether anybody has found the missing plane yet."

Miss Pickerell's thoughts came back to the men of the lost expedition. She hoped the plane had landed safely somewhere. She hoped everybody had survived the experience. She hoped they would be found before it was too late.

She thought of something.

"Mr. Busby," she said, "didn't you say the snowmobile has a short-wave radio? Do you know how to operate it?"

"Naturally," Mr. Busby said. "I'm a sales engineer. I was thinking about that, too, Miss Pickerell. The only thing is, to get inside the snowmobile now, I'd have to disturb the way it's lashed to the pallet with the cargo parachute attached. I think it would be better to leave things just as they are, in case we have to drop the vehicle to the survivors."

"And anyway," said Foster, "we're still a long distance from where the plane has disappeared. We're too far away to hear them even if they are sending out distress signals. We're too far from anybody. The nearest arctic air base is still hundreds of miles away."

At few minutes later Foster brought the plane down, smoothly and without incident, on a flat area of smooth rock that sloped gently out into a small lake.

7

Refueling on the Tundra

As soon as they landed, Foster and Mr. Busby began the preparations for taking the landing wheels off and putting on floats instead.

At first Miss Pickerell didn't see how they could possibly do it. There was nothing to support the plane while they made the exchange. There were no trees—nothing from which the plane could be suspended while they worked—and the plane was certainly much too heavy to be lifted, even if all three of them lifted at once.

But then Miss Pickerell found out what she hadn't known before. The plane had built-in jacks.

Foster had remained inside when she and Mr. Busby got out, and now she saw

him lean down and turn on something below his seat. There was a humming roar
and three sturdy supports, with small
wheels at their ends, were pushed down
from the bottom of the plane. They reached
the ground and continued pushing until the
plane was raised high enough for the landing wheels to be free of the ground. Mr.
Busby piled rocks around the supports so
the plane wouldn't move.

Foster came to the door of the plane,
and Miss Pickerell saw him handing out
the floats to Mr. Bubsy. They were like
small boats, except that they were entirely
enclosed, and were very light. It seemed
to be quite easy for Foster and Mr. Busby
to lift them. They must have been packed
somewhere in the dark enclosed end of the
cabin. Miss Pickerell hadn't noticed them
before.

"Ouch!" Miss Pickerell said. She
slapped her leg where a mosquito had bit-
ten her.

"Good thing we have this stiff breeze,"
Foster said, jumping down to the ground,
"or the mosquitoes would be *really* bad."

"What can I do to help?" Miss Pickerell
asked.

"Nothing till we've done the refueling,"

Mr. Busby said. "But when we get the wheels off, you might prepare them for caching."

"We're not taking the wheels with us?" Miss Pickerell asked.

Foster said, "We can't use landing wheels on either ice or water or deep snow, and it's a good rule in the arctic never to take anything with you that you can do without. On the other hand, though, you have to be sure that you *do* have everything that's necessary."

For a few moments Miss Pickerell watched Foster and Mr. Busby refueling the plane. The barrels of gasoline had been cached in a hollow depression in the rock, with other rocks piled around them so that they wouldn't tip over and blow away.

The refueling was tedious work. First the barrels of gasoline had to be tipped on their sides. Then the gasoline was poured into cans which were light enough to be lifted up to the openings of the gas tanks.

Miss Pickerell walked away and looked about her.

It was certainly true what Foster had said about the ground being damp. After a few squashy steps, Miss Pickerell came back to the rock. Long purple shadows lay across the yellowish-green of the tundra. The air was filled with the cries of the thousands of birds which Miss Pickerell could see running or flying about her in all directions. And everywhere she looked, beautiful gay-colored flowers were blooming.

Miss Pickerell closed her eyes and drew in deep breaths of the crisp clear air.

But suddenly she shivered. The wind had become stronger and more bitter. Her feet were cold and damp, and when she opened her eyes again the whole tundra was one vast purple shadow. Far in the distance she saw an ugly wall of dark gray cloud where, but a moment ago, had shone the beautiful red-gold globe of the sun.

Hugging her elbows to her sides, Miss Pickerell hurried back to the plane.

"Here," Foster said, as he met Miss Pickerell at the door of the plane, "put this parka on. It's one I've had for a long time."

And then he saw Miss Pickerell's wet feet.

"You shouldn't have done that, Miss Pickerell," he said. "You'll have to change your shoes right away. In the arctic, you should never get any part of your body wet if you can possibly help it. You should never overexercise and perspire. And you should always keep your feet dry. If the skin of your body is wet, it makes it a lot harder to get warm again.''

Miss Pickerell took off her hat and put on the parka. The hood was lined with fur. "It tickles," she said.

"That's wolverine fur," said Foster, and he handed her a pair of waterproof skin boots to put on in place of her wet shoes, and a pair of gloves. "When it's very cold the moisture in your breath turns to ice the minute you breathe it out. If your parka hood is lined with any other kind of fur, your breath freezes on the lining and makes your face cold. Wolverine fur is the only kind of fur that your frozen breath doesn't stick to.''

"All right, Miss Pickerell," Mr. Busby called. "We're about ready for you."

He had taken one of the landing wheels off and was rolling it to one side of the plane, where two large pieces of heavy paper were spread out with rocks on their corners to hold them down. He put the wheel in the middle of one of them.

He said, "This is a special kind of paper that gives off a chemical vapor that prevents anything wrapped up in it from rusting. We use it all the time in our factory when we are preparing metal trailer parts for shipping. What you can do, Miss Pickerell, is to see that each wheel is tightly wrapped and that all the seams are sealed with this special tape." He handed her a roll of tape. "With you to help us, we'll be able to get off that much sooner."

"Yes, of course," Miss Pickerell said.

The wind tore at her parka, and it was hard to work with the stiff paper. Even with the gloves on, her fingers grew clumsy and cold, and several times she had to lift one edge of the heavy wheel in order to adjust the paper. But she did not falter. If the weather plane was still missing, if no one had located it yet, every minute might be important. She was glad that she could help.

Mr. Busby and Foster brought her the second wheel, and while she was wrapping it, they took the first one and cached it in a depression in the rock. They covered it with a heavy tarpaulin which they weighted down all around with large stones. They did the same with the second wheel when it was ready for them.

Then they all got back into the plane.

Foster handed Miss Pickerell a pair of loose-fitting skin pants.

"If you put these on under your parka instead of your dress, Miss Pickerell, you'll be a good deal warmer," he said.

When she had changed to the skin pants, Miss Pickerell did not immediately take her seat. She went forward and stood behind Foster, so that she could watch as they took off. Mr. Busby had taken the rocks away that were around the bottoms of the jacks.

Slowly the plane moved forward along the slope of rock toward the lake. The little wheels on the built-in jacks seemed to relay every unevenness on the ground below as they advanced over the edge of the lake and into the water, whose surface was roughened by the wind.

In a few moments the whole weight of the plane was supported on the floats, and Miss Pickerell noticed a very different type of motion—a gentle rocking like that of a boat.

Foster opened the door of the plane and stepped lightly down onto one of the floats, where he lifted a flap on the top of it and looked in.

60

"It's all right," he said as he climbed back into the plane. "I just wanted to make sure I hadn't forgotten the paddles. I always carry paddles inside one of the floats. If something happened so that I had to come down on a lake, and couldn't start my engines again, it might be necessary to paddle in order to get to shore."

He took his place again at the controls and asked Miss Pickerell to go back and fasten herself in her seat.

"I'm pulling up the jacks now," he said, and Miss Pickerell heard the rumble under her feet. The plane built up speed as it skittered across the lake, with the water below them hissing against the floats. Then they were in the air, climbing.

Foster banked the plane and they headed north once more to search for the missing expedition.

8

Will the Weather
Deteriorate?

For the first time Miss Pickerell recalled
the gloomy warning of the man in the
weather station in Square Toe City—that
the weather in the arctic regions might be
going to deteriorate in the next few days.
There was certainly no sign of it that *she*
could see.

Mr. Busby unwrapped another package
of sandwiches and offered one to Miss
Pickerell.

"Too bad Model X24 isn't open," he
said, "or we could cook a regular meal."

Miss Pickerell looked through the dimness to the snowmobile. It was hard to tell exactly what it looked like. Still eating her sandwich, she got up to look at it. She was surprised to see how large the body of it was—almost as large as a house trailer.

Mr. Busby came and stood beside her, and they both held on to the straps that held the vehicle to the pallet, in order to brace themselves against the jouncing of the plane.

"A beauty, isn't she!" said Mr. Busby proudly. "Your cow will be delighted to have it, I'm sure. If we don't have to drop it to the missing men. Here. Take this flashlight. If you stand on your tiptoes and shine it through that window I think you can see in."

Miss Pickerell did so.

"Why," she said over her shoulder, "I had no idea it was so luxurious."

"I'd better check with Foster," Mr. Busby said, "about that air base where we're going to refuel again. I'll ask him for our ETA too."

Miss Pickerell turned around. " 'ETA'?" she asked. "What is that?"

"It's an abbreviation we pilots use,"

"I had no idea it was so luxurious"

said Mr. Busby. "ETA stands for Estimated Time of Arrival."

Miss Pickerell ate the rest of her sandwich. Then she stood on tiptoe again and held the flashlight to the window. She was still looking in when Mr. Busby came back.

"I see the radio set in there," she said. She gave Mr. Busby the flashlight and went back to her seat. "What did Foster say?" she asked. "What is our ETA?"

Mr. Busby did not immediately sit down. He stood in front of Miss Pickerell and looked at her as if he were trying to make up his mind whether or not to tell her something. Then he spoke.

"Foster can't tell our ETA," he said, "because—"

"Is it very far yet?" Miss Pickerell asked. "You and Foster must be terribly tired."

"I'm glad you're a woman of spirit, Miss Pickerell," Mr. Busby said. "What I have to tell you may come as a shock. We may not be able to reach that arctic air base after all."

"You mean we don't have enough fuel to get there?"

"It isn't that," Mr. Busby said. "But Foster has had a good deal of experience

as a bush pilot. He's very familiar with arctic flying conditions, and he says he doesn't
like the looks of the weather in the direction of the air base. In fact, Foster says,
the weather in that direction is deteriorat-
ing rapidly.''

9

Trapped by an Arctic Storm

"Suppose you come forward with me, Miss Pickerell," Mr. Busby said, "and we'll all three talk it over."

But even before Miss Pickerell had quite got out of her seat, the plane gave a wicked lurch and threw her to her knees. Mr. Busby was flung against the side of the plane.

"Strap yourself into your seat, Miss Pickerell," Mr. Busby called out.

He started to fight his way forward, but Foster was calling something to him, and he returned and strapped himself into his own seat. He sat there, with his head

67

turned, watching Foster intently. In between the shattering jolts of the plane,
Miss Pickerell was able to focus her eyes,
and she saw that Mr. Busby had his firm
jaw clamped tightly shut. The muscles of
his neck were stretched taut. He must be
very worried.

Miss Pickerell didn't think he was showing very much confidence in Foster. After
all, Foster was an experienced arctic pilot,
and anybody could tell just by the master-
ful way he was fighting the controls, that
he had the strength and the ability to handle the plane.

For what seemed like a long, long time—
later Miss Pickerell found out it was several hours—the plane struggled through the
wild tossing winds of the storm. With each
lurch, each drop, the plane creaked and
groaned, and the wind constantly roared,
frequently silencing the heavy noise of the
engines.

Miss Pickerell was sore and bruised.
Her back ached, and the seat belt cut into
her each time the plane flung her sideways.

But at last the storm eased. The creaking
and groaning lessened. The roar of the engines penetrated the dying moans of the
wind.

Mr. Busby quickly unstrapped himself and hurried forward.

Miss Pickerell watched, and saw him change places with Foster. Foster, limp and exhausted from his long ordeal, slumped to the floor of the plane and sat there, behind Mr. Busby, with his back braced against the wall.

Miss Pickerell unfastened her strap, found a Thermos bottle, poured out some hot soup and carried it forward to Foster.

Foster took the soup, and as he raised his head and smiled wearily, Miss Pickerell turned and looked over the top of Mr. Busby's head, and out through the window.

"How can it be dark?" Miss Pickerell asked. "It looks just like night out there. But we're supposed to be in the arctic where the summer sun shines twenty-four hours a day. Where in the world are we, anyway?"

"Now don't worry, Miss Pickerell," Mr. Busby said over his shoulder. "Everything is going to be all right."

"Sure," Foster said. He drank some more soup. "It's just that the storm clouds are cutting off the sun. It makes it look dark."

69

"Then I suppose we're flying on instruments," said Miss Pickerell.

"The storm knocked out some of them," Foster said gloomily.

"Now, Foster," Mr. Busby said, "There's no use alarming Miss Pickerell. Everything's going to be all right, isn't it?"

"Sure," Foster said again. But he looked down into his soup as he said it.

"See here!" said Miss Pickerell. "If there's something wrong, I wish you'd tell me. It's always better to know the truth, even if it's bad. That way you know just what to expect and you can prepare yourself for it. When people don't tell you the truth, you get to imagining things, and sometimes what you imagine is worse than the facts."

"Miss Pickerell," Mr. Busby said, "allow me once more to pay tribute to your spirit. The truth is—"

"Let me tell her, Mr. Busby," Foster said. "It's my responsibility. I should have realized sooner that the weather was going to deteriorate. It's this way, Miss Pickerell. If the clouds would just part—if we could just get a glimpse of what is under us—then I'd have some idea of. . . . Well. . . ."

"I wish you'd come right out and tell me," Miss Pickerell said. "I'd rather know the truth, no matter how bad it is. Are *we* lost too?"

Foster looked up. "Of course we're still in the arctic," he said. "But it's impossible to know just how far we were driven by the storm, or in what direction. And unless the storm clouds open up so we can get a sight of the ground, we have no way of telling whether we are over land, or whether we are over open water, or whether we are over ice."

A shiver of fear ran through Miss Pickerell. She remembered the paper-thin floats with which the plane was now equipped.

Foster continued, "Unless we can land on water, there isn't much chance of—"

"Foster!" Mr. Busby shouted, and Foster leaped to his feet.

Mr. Busby said something else, but with his back to her, and with the noise of the plane, Miss Pickerell couldn't hear his words. She saw him stab his finger at one of the instrument dials on the panel before him, and hold up his hand with his thumb and middle finger forming a zero. She saw Foster suck in his breath.

"Miss Pickerell!" Foster shouted.

"We're running out of gasoline. There's only one thing to do now. No matter what's under us, we have to try it. Go to your seat and strap yourself in tightly. I'm going to have to try to make a crash landing."

10

A Crash Landing

After it was all over, after the sickening, crunching, crashing jolt of their landing that threw them forward almost on the plane's nose before they dropped back with a heavy thud, Miss Pickerell sat for an instant utterly unable to move. But it was only the shock. In a moment she was clawing at her seat belt, and the silence which had followed the landing was broken by hoarse male shouts.

"Hurry!" "Get her out quick!" "No time to lose!"

Suddenly Foster and Mr. Busby were beside her, frantically trying to lift her up.

"Let go of me!" Miss Pickerell said, shaking her arm free. "I can get out by myself."

"Well, hurry up then!" said Mr. Busby. He pushed open the shattered door and jumped out. Miss Pickerell followed, with Foster close behind her.

"Over here," Foster called, wading through loose snow to a point some distance from the plane. Miss Pickerell and Mr. Busby joined him.

"What was all the rush?" Miss Pickerell asked. "We'd have been a good deal more comfortable inside, I should think. I'm cold."

"Then put up the hood of your parka, Miss Pickerell," said Foster.

And Mr. Busby said, "The rush was on account of fire. There's always danger of fire in a crash landing of this kind. We had to get away to safety, just in case."

"Oh," said Miss Pickerell. "I'm sorry I spoke like that."

For a few moments they stood in silence, looking at the wrecked plane. Miss Pickerell could hear heavy breathing and it was a while before she realized that it was her own. The parka around her head seemed to make her breathing sound loud. When she looked at Foster and Mr. Busby, they too were panting, either from the exertion of fleeing from the plane or perhaps as a reaction from the shock of the crash landing.

Foster and Mr. Busby looked at each other, and Mr. Busby said, "We'll open the snowmobile and start the heater in it. The heater runs on batteries."

"Wait," Foster said. "You and Miss Pickerell stay here while I make an inspection."

Miss Pickerell looked about her.

Suddenly she realized something. And now that she had noticed it, it seemed funny that it hadn't occurred to her before.

"Why!" she said. "We came down on land. We didn't land on open water at all."

Mr. Busby drew her attention to the shattered floats beneath the plane, and pointed to the two tracks they had made deep in the snow. The tracks began at the edge of a small area of windswept ice. He whistled with surprise and admiration.

"Here's what must have happened," he said, "and I ought to tell you, Miss Pickerell, that few pilots could have made such a brilliant landing. Obviously, when we got down through the clouds, Foster spotted this one tiny bare patch of ice. He knew

75

that our one chance was to land here. And somehow he was skillful enough to do just that. Although the ice tore our floats to pieces, it was the only thing that could have saved us."

"I think I understand," Miss Pickerell said. "If we had landed in the snow, the snow would have stopped us suddenly and turned us upside down."

"We'd have been lucky to get out alive," said Mr. Busby. "But when Foster landed us on the ice, most of our speed was absorbed by the time we slithered into the snow."

Miss Pickerell scraped away the loose snow with the toe of her skin boot. Since the fur side of the skin was on the inside of the boots, it didn't make her feet cold to do this. She scraped away the snow in several other places and in each case she found ice. She wondered if they might have landed on a glacier.

Foster came to the door of the plane and Miss Pickerell and Mr. Busby joined him.

Foster leaned down and ruefully examined the wrecked floats. From the expression on his face it was easy to see his disappointment.

"I thought there was just a chance that the things inside the floats would still be intact," he said, reaching into the wreckage.

"But—" said Miss Pickerell, remembering how Foster had checked to see if he had paddles inside the floats. "But what good would paddles do us now?"

Foster straightened up. He held in his hand a twisted mass of leather thongs and shattered wood.

"I had these in the other float," he said. "Snowshoes. They would have come in pretty handy. In case we aren't rescued. In case I have to go somewhere for help."

"Well, for mercy's sakes!" Miss Pickerell said. "Why would you go anywhere on snowshoes when we have a fully equipped snowmobile—and the latest model at that? The only reason we brought it was so it could be used for rescue work if it was needed."

"I guess you've forgotten something, Miss Pickerell," said Foster.

"Yes," said Mr. Busby. "The reason we had to land was that we're out of gasoline."

"But isn't there any for the snowmobile?" Miss Pickerell asked.

Mr. Busby shook his head, and Foster looked away.

For a moment they were all silent, and each of them knew that the others were thinking the same thing. Now there were *two* planes down in the arctic. The work of the rescuers had been made twice as hard.

"Come on, Foster," said Mr. Busby. "Let's uncrate the snowmobile so we can get at the radio and send out a distress signal."

As soon as the straps had been unfastened on one side of the snowmobile, they all went inside it. Miss Pickerell found it to be just like a very well-planned home. Everything was compact and convenient. In one end were three bunks, one above the other. The opposite end was for cooking and eating, and she found the supply cupboards were fully stocked with food. Just below the window on one of the side walls was the radio set.

Mr. Busby had started the heater and the whole enclosure began to glow with welcome warmth. He and Foster went to the radio, and Miss Pickerell set about fixing a hot meal for them all, which they ate sitting around a small table in the corner.

"The radio's automatic SOS signal is on," said Mr. Busby. "Any pilot who flies near us is bound to hear it."

Foster said nothing. He kept right on chewing rather slowly and looking down at the floor.

Mr. Busby leaned back comfortably on his stool and wiped his mouth with a bright red paper napkin. "You certainly cook a delicious meal, Miss Pickerell," he said. "And now if you'll excuse me, I'll go back to the radio set and listen. As soon as a pilot picks up our signal, I'll talk to him. Maybe he can tell us about the fate of the other plane, too."

Foster stopped chewing entirely and looked up.

"I'd better tell you both," he said, "that I'm afraid nobody is going to pick up our signal. You see, unless we were spotted, nobody knows we're missing. I didn't file a flight plan."

"You didn't!" said Mr. Busby. "Tch! Tch!"

"I know," said Foster. "I know a pilot should always file a flight plan, and then close it when he arrives where he is going. But I didn't do it this time on purpose. When someone files a flight plan and then doesn't close it, for any reason at all, rescue planes have to go out and search for him, because he *might* be in trouble. I was afraid that if we got delayed for some reason, they might think *we* were in trouble. That would mean that half of the search planes which are looking for the other expedition would have to come and look for us. I know it was very unwise of me."

Miss Pickerell agreed privately. At the same time, she admired the generous reason that had kept Foster from filing a flight plan.

"And not only that," said Foster. "I have no way of knowing just where we are. It may be that the storm drove us to an entirely different part of the arctic."

Mr. Busby said, "I'll draw up a schedule for monitoring the radio set. One of us will have to be there at all times. To answer— in case a plane or some air base or radio station *does* pick up our signal for help. I'm afraid we'll have to call on you to take your turn, Miss Pickerell."

"Well, I should hope so," said Miss Pickerell. She tried to speak brightly, but she knew perfectly well—and she knew that Foster and Mr. Busby knew too—that they were in a very serious situation.

Mr. Busby snapped into action. "Now then," he said, "let's not waste any time."

Foster stood up quickly. "I'll go out and tramp a big SOS in the snow," he said. "Also I have some bright-colored fluorescent strips of cloth to use for markers to draw attention to the plane—in case anybody *does* come near us."

"I'll come and help you," said Miss Pickerell.

11

The Lost Expedition

Miss Pickerell thought it was very interesting the way they put out the bright-colored cloth markers.

There were two of them, shaped in the form of arrows. Foster laid them both out on the ice. Then he moved them around until the points of both arrows were pointing toward the plane.

He gave Miss Pickerell a sharp knife and showed her how to help him anchor the markers. He showed her how to use the knife to cut two holes in the ice about six inches apart and slanting in toward each other so that they met at the bottom. This formed a solid arch of ice. The markers had cords at the corners, and it was a simple matter to tie the cords to the arches of ice.

"Now," said Foster, "we'll go and tramp down a big SOS in the snow."

By the time they had finished this, Miss Pickerell was so tired she ached all over.

They took off their snowy outer garments in the body of the airplane, for Foster too had put on a parka and skin boots and gloves. As soon as they entered the warm snowmobile, Miss Pickerell insisted that both men go to their berths and get some sleep, for she knew they both must be a good deal more tired than she was. She would monitor the radio set if they would show her how.

She already knew a little bit about what to do because of having watched Dwight and Rosemary so many times.

"Put on the earphones," Foster said "and flick this key by the mouthpiece. Keep listening all the time. If you hear anybody, wake us up immediately."

Miss Pickerell was glad to find that the cord of the headphones was long enough to allow her to clear the table and wash the dishes and still listen at the same time. It would have been very monotonous if she just had to sit there. Foster had chopped out a large block of ice and it had melted in the large kettle on the stove, so she had plenty of water for dishwashing.

After she finished the dishes, she unrolled the sleeping bag that Rosemary had packed for her. One of the men had brought it inside the snowmobile and put it in one corner. Rosemary had done a wonderful job of packing. She had put in everything that Miss Pickerell might possibly need—including a pair of dark glasses and even Rosemary's own camera in case Miss Pickerell wanted to take some pictures.

Miss Pickerell put the things in the bunk that had been left for her, and was very quiet about it so as not to disturb the sleeping men.

Then she sat down in front of the set. She was determined to keep her vigil here just as long as she possibly could without going to sleep. Of course if she began to get too sleepy, she would *have* to wake someone up to take her place. It wouldn't be safe otherwise. She might go to sleep and not hear someone talking on the radio.

In spite of all she could do, her head began to nod. Suddenly there was a voice in her earphones! She jumped up. "Mr. Busby!" she shouted. "Foster! Wake up!"

The voice was quite distinct. It was exactly as though someone were speaking on the telephone.

There was a thud of stockinged feet on the floor, and just before Foster snatched off her earphones, Miss Pickerell heard the voice say, "Rescue plane to lost weather expedition. Rescue plane to lost weather expedition. Do you read? Over."

Almost shaking with eagerness, Foster sat down and pressed the key beside the mouthpiece.

"Calling rescue plane," he said. "Calling rescue plane. Over." Then he listened.

Miss Pickerell and Mr. Busby stood right behind him, hardly breathing.

Again Foster spoke into the mouthpiece and listened. And again. And again. It was no use.

"They don't hear us," he said sadly, pushing back one of the earphones so that he could listen to the radio and talk to Miss Pickerell and Mr. Busby at the same time. "What do you make of it, Mr. Busby?"

"Probably our transmitter doesn't have enough power to reach them," Mr. Busby said. "What are they saying?"

"They just keep repeating, 'Rescue plane to lost weather expedition.' I can't tell from that whether the expedition has been found or not. Maybe the expedition has been found and they are trying to contact them with a further message—Wait!" He clapped the other earphone tight against his ear and sat hunched over, intently listening. Miss Pickerell was so excited she could hardly stand waiting to find out what was being said.

Foster reached for a pencil and began making rapid notes on a piece of paper in front of him. Looking over his shoulder, Miss Pickerell saw the notes were figures of latitude and longitude.

Finally Foster straightened up. He tried once more to make himself heard on the radio but there was no response. He turned around.

"That was the weather expedition," he said. "And this is their location." He put his pencil on the figures.

"How are they?" Miss Pickerell asked. "Are they all right?"

"The pilot was very badly injured," said Foster, "and needs medical attention. The plane crashed in an area of jagged crevasses, and the rescue plane can't make a landing there. The man is too badly hurt to be carried out by stretcher. The rescue plane has a very powerful radio set and is going to radio for a doctor and a helicopter. But the nearest air base is far away, and it will be a long time before help can reach them. The rescue plane is going to stand by as long as its fuel lasts."

"Oh, that poor man!" Miss Pickerell said. And she knew Foster and Mr. Busby had the same thought.

"Let me take the earphones, Foster," Mr. Busby said. "I'll keep trying to contact the plane at thirty-second intervals. If the other plane that's wrecked *is* anywhere near, there's a chance the rescue plane might hear us."

Foster got up and changed places with Mr. Busby. He picked up the sheet of paper with the figures of the other plane's location. "If I could only figure out *our* position, I could tell how far away we are from them." He stood thinking for a moment, and then he said, "I'm going into the cockpit of the plane and make some calculations. I might just possibly be able to tell."

He had been gone only a few minutes, when he scurried back inside the snowmobile. "I did it," he said. "I've calculated our position. Look, Mr. Busby."

Mr. Busby uncovered one ear as Foster spoke.

Foster put the two sets of figures down side by side in front of Mr. Busby.

"See, Mr. Busby," he said. "Our longitude is the same as theirs. And there's just a very little difference in our latitude. We're just a little bit north of them."

Foster turned around. "I suppose you know, Miss Pickerell, that latitude and longitude give the location of places on the surface of the earth. The figures for longitude show how far east or west anything is. The figures for latitude tell how far north or south. According to these two sets of figures, we're directly north of the other expedition, and not very far away at that."

"We could rescue the injured man," Mr. Busby said, "if we only had fuel for the snowmobile. We could drive in, get him, and bring him out to some place where the rescue plane could land."

"But what about the crevasses?" Miss Pickerell asked.

Mr. Busby said, "The big tread around the two back wheels on each side is long enough so that the vehicle can cross over a narrow crevasse without falling in. Foster, did the expedition say anything about whether they were out of gas?"

"It was the storm that made them crash," Foster said. "Not lack of fuel."

Suddenly Miss Pickerell saw what Mr. Busby was getting at.

"If you'll tell me which way to go, Foster," he said, "I'll go to that other expedition and bring back some gasoline."

Foster responded quickly. "I'll go with you," he said. "I'm more familiar with the arctic and perhaps I can help the survivors in some way. You don't mind, do you, Miss Pickerell?"

"Well, of *course* not," Miss Pickerell said. "Here, give me the earphones, Mr. Busby."

The two men dressed themselves warmly. They not only wore parkas, but each of them also put on a pair of loose-fitting skin pants, with the fur inside. Mr. Busby didn't have any dark glasses, so Miss Pickerell let him have the pair that Rosemary had put in her pack.

She found that by stretching the cord of the earphones as far as it would go, she could step outside of the snowmobile and watch through the battered door of the

She could watch through the battered door

plane as Mr. Busby and Foster grew
smaller and smaller in the distance. She
noticed that they went in single file through
the snow so that they would not waste their
energy in breaking two separate trails.

She went back inside the snowmobile
and shut the door. She began to set the

table so that when the men returned she wouldn't need to lose any time in getting them something to eat. And then, suddenly, she was sleepy again. So sleepy she could hardly stand it. It must have been the excitement that had kept her awake until now.

If she only had something absorbing to occupy her mind that might keep her awake. She wished now that Rosemary had included some of the famous rocks that Miss Pickerell had brought back with her from her trip to Mars. She could spend the time studying the rocks and reclassifying them. But she didn't have the rocks and her head began to nod.

Then she snapped wide awake. A voice was speaking in her earphones!

12

Miss Pickerell
Makes Contact

"Rescue plane to weather expedition. Rescue plane to weather expedition," the voice was saying. "Over."

Miss Pickerell dashed to the radio set and pressed the key beside the mouthpiece as she sat down.

"Hello!" she said. "Hello! Over." And she released the key.

Nothing happened. She didn't even hear the other voice this time.

Oh, surely he couldn't have gone too far away to hear her! He couldn't have turned off his set so soon!

She tried again. Perhaps she should

identify herself in some way. She pressed the key.

"Hello," she said. "Snowmobile expedition to rescue plane. Snowmobile expedition to rescue plane. Come in please. Over."

This time there was an immediate response.

"Rescue plane to—Repeat that please. Over."

Miss Pickerell again spoke into the mouthpiece.

"Snowmobile expedition to rescue plane. Over."

"Where are you, snowmobile expedition. Are you in trouble? Over."

Miss Pickerell explained what had happened—how they had come to the arctic in the first place because they hoped to be able to help in locating and perhaps rescuing the missing weather expedition, how they themselves had had to make a crash landing, and how Foster had figured out their latitude and longitude. She read the figures to the unseen man in the air, from the slip of paper Foster had left at the radio set.

"Mmm," the man said. He seemed to

be checking something. "You aren't very
far from where I am right now."

Miss Pickerell explained to the man how
Foster and Mr. Busby had gone to get
some fuel for the snowmobile so that they
could rescue the wounded pilot.

"Too bad," the man said. "I have a
drum of gasoline I can drop to you. Maybe
they'll turn around when they hear my
plane. What is the condition of the snow
where you are?"

Miss Pickerell thought this was a funny
thing to ask if he was just going to drop
something by parachute, but she said,
"Hold the line a minute," and left the cozy
warmth of the snowmobile and looked out
through the door of the airplane. Then she
hurried back to the snowmobile, leaned
toward the mouthpiece, and spoke to the
man.

"There's a big drift of snow on the left-
hand side of the plane. Over."

"I've used up all my parachutesfor the
other wrecked plane," the voice said. "But
the gasoline drum was sealed up only 90
per cent full so it would be safe to drop it
in a snowdrift without a parachute. I'll
have to come in at about fifty feet."

*"In the middle of this snowdrift there is a
drum of gasoline"*

At that moment Miss Pickerell heard, in her free ear, a faint hum in the air above her. It grew louder.

"We see you, snowmobile expedition," the voice said. The man didn't say "Over"; so Miss Pickerell didn't flick the key. She kept listening tensely.

The roaring grew louder. And lower. And closer.

"Coming in, snowmobile expedition,"

said the voice. Then the loud roaring seemed to whoosh right across the top of the plane, and the voice said, "Drums away!"

Then the voice said, "I see the other members of your expedition. They're turning back. I'll tell the other expedition that you are coming in your snowmobile to rescue the injured man. I'llcontact you again in about thirty minutes to tell you where to bring him, so that I can land and pick him up. Over."

It probably wasn't very long, but it *seemed* like a long time before Mr. Busby and Foster returned and found Miss Pickerell in her boots and parka wading in the snowdrift.

"Miss Pickerell!" Mr. Busby shouted angrily, as soon as he was near enough. "Why aren't you inside at the radio set! Why aren't you trying to contact that plane instead of letting it get away from us. They might have been able to spare us some gasoline. How could you do such a thing!"

Miss Pickerell was unperturbed. "Somewhere in the middle of this snowdrift," she said, "there is a drum of gasoline for our snowmobile.'' And she went on to explain all that had happened.

"I guess our troubles are over now," she said.

But Miss Pickerell was mistaken about that.

13

Model X24 to the Rescue

Foster had lost no time, after Miss Pickerell's explanation, in looking for the drum.
"Here it is," he called from the middle of
the snowdrift. "Here's the drum of gasoline."

After they had poured the gasoline into
the snowmobile's tank, Foster and Mr.
Busby pried open the cargo hatch of the
airplane and lowered the top of it to the
ground. The bottom was hinged and supported in such a way that it provided a
sloping ramp for the snowmobile. Fortunately, that part of the plane had not been
damaged.

Getting the snowmobile out presented a
slight problem, however, because instead

of front wheels there were two skis. Miss Pickerell made a suggestion.

"Why don't we scoop up a lot of snow and pack it under the skis," she said, "and down across the ramp. Then the snowmobile can drive right out onto the ground. We can use the empty fuel drum to scoop the snow with."

This proved to be all that was necessary. With Foster and Miss Pickerell standing at one side watching tensely, Mr. Busby climbed into the cab of the snowmobile, started the engine, and slowly drove the vehicle out through the cargo hatch and down the snowpacked ramp.

Miss Pickerell held her breath and bit the corner of her lip, she was so nervous. If anything happened so the snowmobile wouldn't work, when the rescue of the poor injured man depended on it. . . .

But she needn't have worried. The caterpillar tread on each side around the two rear wheels made it possible for the snowmobile to negotiate easily the slight bump at the end of the ramp.

Foster and Miss Pickerell got in beside Mr. Busby, with Miss Pickerell in the middle, and they started out. The snowmobile crunched powerfully and steadily across the drifts of snow and areas of windswept ice. At first they were all so tense and worried about the injured man that no one said anything.

But then Foster began to talk, as if to keep them from worrying so much. He began to tell them some of his bush pilot experiences. He told them about once when his plane had been wrecked because of the white-out.

"What's that?" Miss Pickerell wanted to know.

"White-out," Foster said, "is when the light conditions are such that the white sky and the white ground look just exactly the same. There are no shadows and no horizon. It's a frightful experience. There's no way to tell where you are. There might be a deep crevasse right in front of you and you wouldn't be able to tell it was there. It's bad enough when you are on the ground during a white-out. But it's even more dangerous in a plane because you can't judge your position in relation to the ground."

After a while Miss Pickerell said, "How do we know we are going in the right direction? I notice the sun is right ahead of us again. How do we know we aren't going north?"

"It's twelve o'clock noon," Foster said. "If we go straight toward the sun we're bound to be going south."

"How do we know it isn't twelve o'clock midnight?" Miss Pickerell asked.

"It's noon all right," Foster said easily. "Although the sun looks low in the sky, it's really higher above the horizon than it is at midnight when it's around to the north."

Miss Pickerell noticed something. "Way over there on the right there's a funny dark smudge on the horizon," she said.

Foster looked where she was pointing.

"What is it, Foster?" Mr. Busby asked.

"It looks like a cloud," Miss Pickerell said. "A low cloud of vapor."

"It's vapor all right," said Foster. "But it isn't a cloud. In the arctic you only see vapor low in the sky like that when there's a break in the surface of the ice. The air over open water has moisture in it. But when the colder air from over the ice comes in contact with the moist air, it cools it. The colder it gets the less moisture it can hold, and the moisture condenses out in the form of vapor or fog.''

''But if there's water under the ice—'' Miss Pickerell said, and suddenly she was frightened. ''Does that mean,'' she asked in a low voice, ''that this glacier, or whatever it is we're on, is right out over the Arctic Ocean?''

''What we're on is called an ice shelf,'' Foster said. ''And the other plane was wrecked on what is known as an ice cap.'' He went on to explain that the ice cap was an enormous, ancient sort of glacier formed of the hard-packed snow that had fallen for tens of thousands of years over a large area on the edge of the Arctic Ocean. He told her that the ice cap was so large and so heavy that part of it had spread right out over the ocean, although it was still connected to the ice cap. That part was the ice shelf, and that was where they were.

Foster looked at his watch. ''It's about time for the rescue plane to contact us,'' he said.

Mr. Busby stopped the snowmobile.

Foster said, ''I'll drive while you are inside at the radio, Mr. Busby. I've driven snowmobiles in the arctic before.''

''A good idea,'' Mr. Busby said, as he

slid back into the snowmobile. "So we won't waste any time. I'll call when I've got through talking to the rescue plane and know what the arrangements are to be."

Miss Pickerell was still interested in what Foster had been telling her. "Is that where icebergs come from? From ice caps and ice shelves?"

"Icebergs come from what are called *living* glaciers," Foster said. "They keep cracking off all the time. Each year more snow piles up on the glacier and packs down and freezes. That weight keeps pressing on the glacier and forcing it down to the sea. An ice cap is much older than a glacier and much more enormous. An ice cap is left over from a time when ice covered a large part of the world. The ice shelf of an ice cap doesn't very often break off. But when it does, it's called an ice island, and drifts slowly around the Arctic Ocean, going from east to west. It might take it several years to get back to where it started."

"I should think it would be melted by that time," Miss Pickerell said.

"Too big," said Foster. "It might be several miles across. Besides that, it would be composed of a very dense kind of ice."

Mr. Busby knocked on the window behind them. As Foster stopped the snowmobile, Miss Pickerell noticed that they must be almost off the ice shelf. Ahead of them, the white vastness of the ice cap rose more steeply, and even from here its surface looked rough and jagged.

"Here's what we're supposed to do," Mr. Busby said when he joined them. "The rescue plane has landed as close to the wreck as it safely can. It didn't want to keep on flying around and using up fuel unnecessarily. We're to rescue the injured man and take him across the crevasses to the plane. He'll be evacuated immediately. Then we'll come back for the others. Two more rescue planes are now on their way. They will pick up the other survivors after we get them out. And us, too, of course. Why, what are you doing, Miss Pickerell?"

"Getting some of my things out of the snowmobile. If I stay here, you'll have more room for the survivors, won't you?"

"That's right," Foster agreed. "We hate to leave you, Miss Pickerell, but—"

"Just hand out my sleeping bag, will you, Foster, so I'll have something dry to sit on. And my umbrella to shade me from the sun." At the last minute, she decided

106

to take Rosemary's camera too. She would take some pictures while she was waiting. They would make a nice souvenir for Dwight and Rosemary.

"Good-by, Miss Pickerell," Foster said, climbing back into the cab of the snow-mobile.

"We'll come for you as soon as we can," said Mr. Busby.

The first thing Miss Pickerell did was to spread out her sleeping bag and sit down on it while she took several pictures of the snowmobile and the forbidding ice cap beyond it. She was glad to see that the snow-mobile did not falter. Occasionally it made a zigzag in its course, as though Mr. Busby were trying to find a narrow part of a crevasse to cross.

Miss Pickerell had opened her umbrella and left it lying upside down in the snow while she took the pictures. When she went to get it she found that the snow, where the umbrella touched it, had begun to melt. It was some little time before she figured out why this was. But eventually she reasoned it out.

Wherever the sun shone directly on the snow there was so much brightness that the sun's rays were reflected back into the

She left the umbrella upside down in the snow

sky again. The umbrella was so dark that it didn't reflect the sun's rays. It absorbed them, which made the cloth warmer. The heat of the cloth then melted the snow underneath.

Miss Pickerell squinted up her eyes from time to time to watch the progress of the snowmobile. Her eyes were beginning to hurt from the glare, for she had not asked Mr. Busby to return her dark glasses. He would need them more than she did.

She lay down on the sleeping bag, turned over on her stomach, and went to sleep. In spite of the snow and ice all around her, the sun shining on her back kept her feeling warm and cozy.

When she wakened and sat up, the snowmobile was out of sight. She could neither see nor hear it. She was utterly alone in the vastness and the silence. She felt strangely exultant. She could understand now why people like Foster loved the arctic—the cleanness and the beauty and the stillness. Most of all the stillness. Miss Pickerell had never imagined there could be such silence.

And into this silence, without warning, came a noise that tore her ears, froze her blood, and made her heart stand still. The surface under her moved with a sickening feeling like an earthquake, and with a roaring, cracking, popping wrench, the ice shelf broke off!

A mile-wide wave of blue water rose slowly through the crack and dashed itself to whiteness in the air.

Miss Pickerell was adrift on an arctic ice island!

14

Adrift in the Arctic Ocean

As fast as she could, Miss Pickerell hurried to the edge of the ice island and looked across the gradually widening water that separated her from the vast ice cap ahead.

As far as she could see, in each direction, the shoreline opposite her, where the massive ice island had broken off, was a smooth cliff of crystal blue. There were strange dark horizontal streaks in the face of the cliff.

Looking down, Miss Pickerell saw that the top of the ice island was only about ten feet above the surface of the water, and it frightened her for a moment because it made the ice island seem so thin and weak. But then she remembered that when ice is floating, there is about eight times as much of it under the water as there is showing. The ice under her feet must be at least ninety feet deep. And Foster had said the ice in an ice island was dense and strong.

After her first shock, Miss Pickerell realized that she was in no great danger. When Foster and Mr. Busby came back for her, they would see what had happened, and if she had drifted out of sight, they would send one of the rescue planes to pick her up.

But the prospect was frightening. Miss Pickerell did not like the idea of being all alone—perhaps for hours—on a platform of ice slowly moving through the Arctic Ocean. Besides that, it would certainly delay the rescue operations for the men of the other plane, the men who had been down so much longer and who had suffered so much more than she had.

She must try to rescue herself, if possible.

She walked along the edge for a few minutes and then she saw something hopeful. The space of open water was slowly filling with huge irregular chunks of ice. The wind was blowing them together. She knew these chunks of ice must be pack ice. They looked rough and coarse, and they seemed almost porous compared with the clear dense ice on which she was standing. One of the pieces of pack ice made a cold tinkling sound as the wind kicked it against the base of the ice island at her feet. Perhaps enough of the pack ice would be blown together to form a bridge on which she could cross.

While she was waiting for this to happen, she went back and got her sleeping bag, her camera, and her umbrella. She took several pictures of the ice and water below her, and of the cliff beyond.

Miss Pickerell drew the hood of her parka tighter about her head. The wind had changed direction, and she saw now that all the drifting pieces of ice were being driven toward the shore. All except the one at the foot of the island. It still knocked and tinkled against the base, apparently shielded from the wind by the height of the island.

She would not be able to cross on the pack ice after all! She must think of something else.

And now her eyes were beginning to pain her from the brightness. She must protect them in some way. Perhaps she should rip the black cloth from her umbrella and make a sort of blindfold with tiny holes punched in it to look through. That might ease the pain. She stooped over to pick up the umbrella and as she did so, she looked down. The stranded piece of ice was still there, directly below, and like a flash Miss Pickerell saw what she must do.

She looked back and forth until she found a place where the broken cliff beneath her was jagged enough to provide a few rough footholds.

Clutching her umbrella, and fastening the camera around her neck by its strap, Miss Pickerell began to descend.

She was fervently glad now that she had not ripped off the cloth.

For the bold plan which had now formed in Miss Pickerell's mind, her umbrella would be indispensable.

15

A Daring Attempt

Making a quick mental calculation, based on how much of the piece of pack ice was showing above the water, Miss Pickerell estimated that it must be well over two feet thick. Surely it was strong enough for what she had in mind!

She stepped down on it. She was right. It supported her weight. She crouched down to avoid tipping over.

She wished now that she had thrown down her sleeping bag before she had clambered down the rough edge of the ice island, so that she would have it to protect her from the cold of the ice beneath her. But to go back again was impossible. And anyway her parka was so long and loose that she could spread it part way under her when she kneeled.

Crouching on her knees, Miss Pickerell reached out and touched the base of the ice island with her closed umbrella. Shoving with all her strength, she pressed sharply on the curved handle. Just as she had hoped it would, the piece of ice shot out into the open water far enough so that the island no longer protected it from the wind.

She was now in the path of the wind, and it began to blow her piece of ice slowly toward the shore.

Miss Pickerell now put the rest of her plan into operation. She must take full advantage of the wind. It might die down, or change direction, at any moment and leave her stranded.

Turning around on her knees, Miss Pickerell opened her umbrella and held it before her, so that it caught the full force of the wind. Immediately she felt the increased speed of the piece of ice.

Every so often Miss Pickerell peeked around the edge of the umbrella to see how much farther she had to go. She did this carefully, holding on to the umbrella handle with both hands. She couldn't take the chance of having the umbrella blown out of her grasp. She was very glad the handle had a curve in it. It made it easier to hang on to.

Now she was more than half way across the open sea. The water became a little rougher and the wind pulled a little more strongly. And then suddenly the wind lessened. The ice began to go more slowly. The wind was dying down!

If only there were some way she could make herself go faster!

Miss Pickerell looked again toward shore. The wind was still weak. She wished there were some way she could take full advantage of what little wind there was. The black cloth was so very thin that some of the wind was blowing right through it. If only it were thicker. If only it could offer full resistance to the wind!

Miss Pickerell had an idea.

Holding very tightly to the handle, she dipped the umbrella over the side of the ice and rotated it in the water until all of the fabric was soaking wet.

When she lifted it out and placed it in front of her again, it behaved just the way she had hoped it would. The wet fabric now made a solid barrier against the wind;

the piece of ice moved faster; the shore came closer; and Miss Pickerell began to look for the rough jagged place in the cliff that matched the place where she had climbed down from the ice island.

It was slightly to one side of the direction in which she was being blown, but she found that by shifting the angle of the umbrella she could alter her course slightly.

Suddenly there was a tinkling bump. She had reached the shore!

Miss Pickerell had maneuvered the piece of ice so well that she was exactly below the rough place in the cliff of ice. She lowered her umbrella. But now that it was so stiff and wet it would not close all the way.

At first it looked impossible to climb the cliff, even here. But then Miss Pickerell saw one jagged irregular place, larger than the others, right above her head. Reaching up, she hooked the umbrella handle behind this place. This gave her something to pull against and she was able to climb that far. From then on it was easy.

Panting from the exertion, weak from the danger through which she had passed, and shaking from the cold, Miss Pickerell started immediately in the direction that the snowmobile had taken. It had left two wide, heavily packed tracks that were very easy to walk in.

Miss Pickerell hurried forward.

And then she stopped just in time.

There was a deep crevasse at her feet. The snowmobile had been able to cross it, but it was too wide for Miss Pickerell to try to jump. She could not go straight ahead. She would have to go around.

She turned aside. She took two floundering steps in the loose snow, and then she faltered. Something was wrong.

The crevasse had disappeared. The tracks of the snowmobile had disappeared. There were no shadows. There was no horizon. There was no earth and no sky. There was nothing. She was lost. With her eyes wide open she was lost.

Miss Pickerell was experiencing the dreaded white-out that Foster had told about. And somewhere near, perhaps only inches away, was the deep yawning emptiness of the crevasse.

She knew she would have to stay here until the white-out ended. Until then she knew it would not be safe to take a single step.

She poked the partly closed umbrella into the snow, hoping that its point would strike the ice and give her something to lean against. But the wind caught the umbrella in such a way that it blew it open again. Hanging onto it in the wind made it very difficult for Miss Pickerell to keep her balance. She dared not hold it. It might blow her into the crevasse, and she let it go.

Then, a moment later, the white-out was over.

Miss Pickerell blinked her eyes. She could see again.

She saw the crevasse with its sheer blue depths only six inches away from her right foot, and instinctively she drew back. She saw the snow. She saw the sky. And she saw something else.

On the other side of the crevasse, she saw a man on snowshoes. He was wearing a flier's leather jacket and he was waving and shouting something to her as he hurried forward. He pointed to the left, and Miss Pickerell stumbled weakly in the direction indicated.

They met at the end of the crevasse.

16

Safe at Last

Now that the suspense was all over, Miss Pickerell suddenly found that she couldn't stand up any more. She felt very silly about it, but she had to accept the man's help when he offered to hold her up.

When he spoke, Miss Pickerell recognized his voice.

"You're the pilot," she said. "The pilot of the rescue plane that I was talking to."

"Co-pilot," said the man. "Co-pilot and drop master. I'm responsible for dropping supplies. The pilot stayed with the plane when we landed in order to maintain radio contact with the wrecked plane and with the snowmobile. But I thought I'd do a little exploring. If we ever had to rescue anybody around here again, it would be helpful to know the country. Do you feel better now? Are you able to walk?"

"I guess so," Miss Pickerell said.

"It won't take us very long to reach the rescue plane," the man said. "It's not very far away, but we can't see it because there's a big hump of ice in the way."

He insisted on taking off his snowshoes and giving them to Miss Pickerell, and while he was fastening them to her feet, she told him everything that had happened since Mr. Busby and Foster had gone ahead to rescue the injured man.

"I was afraid that if I stayed on the ice island, you'd have to rescue me too, and it might delay things for the other survivors."

"You were quite right," the co-pilot said. "I heard that tremendous crash and I guessed what had happened. I wish I could have seen it happening. It's a very rare occurrence, you know, for an ice island to break off. I wish I could have got some pictures of it. Now then, I guess we're ready. Just follow the tracks I made. I'll be right behind you."

It took Miss Pickerell awhile to get used to the snowshoes. They were so wide and long, but they did give her feet a nice support. They kept her walking on the surface of the snow, instead of sinking in with each step.

The man had sounded so wistful when he spoke about wishing he could have got some pictures that Miss Pickerell told him about the pictures she had taken with Rosemary's camera. "If they turn out well," she said, "I'll send you some. Oh, look! There's your plane!" They had just come around the base of an enormous sloping hump of ice. In the middle of a wide flat area was the plane. Miss Pickerell noticed it was equipped with skis for landing on snow.

"Yes," said the co-pilot close behind her, "and there's the snowmobile too. Just coming into sight, off there to the left."

The snowmobile reached the plane before they did, however, and Miss Pickerell and the co-pilot arrived just as four men were tenderly lifting the injured man, on an improvised stretcher, into the rescue plane. Two of them were Foster and Mr. Busby.

Foster and Mr. Busby were quite surprised when they saw Miss Pickerell, but nobody had time for any explanations. It was quickly decided that Foster and Miss Pickerell should fly out with the injured

man and the other two men who had come in the snowmobile. The more people who went, the fewer trips the other rescue planes would have to make.

In the meantime, Mr. Busby would go back with the snowmobile and evacuate the other survivors.

As soon as the plane had taken off, everyone set about making the injured man more comfortable. Miss Pickerell helped as much as she could. Soon he felt so much better that he was able to talk. He and the other two members of the expedition began to discuss the purpose of their trip to the arctic.

Miss Pickerell remembered the newspaper article she had started to read to Rosemary that night in her kitchen. The

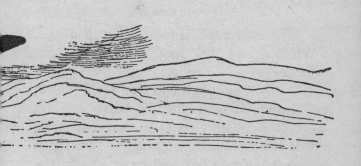

article had said that this expedition was
going to make a different kind of weather
observation from the kind that was usually
made. She asked the men about it.

"Yes," one of them said. "We were
going to establish ourselves on a glacier
and bore holes into it as deep as we could
so that there would be a long round core.
Then we would pull out this core and study
it."

"Whatever for?" Miss Pickerell asked. "What would that have to do with the weather?"

"It might have a lot to do," said the injured man. It seemed to be better for him to talk. He didn't seem to think so much about his injuries then. "If we knew enough about what weather had been like in the past, we might be able to detect some kind of a pattern that repeats itself over and over. There might be a certain number of years with severe winters, and then a certain number of years with mild weather. If that happened often enough, we might expect the same thing to happen in the future."

"I still don't see," said Miss Pickerell, "how you could tell that by boring a hole in a glacier."

One of the other men explained. "On a glacier," he said, "the snow that falls doesn't melt away completely. Each year's snow just piles up on the snow that fell the winter before and packs it down into ice. But between each winter, in the summer when it isn't snowing, any debris or dust in the atmosphere would settle on the surface. It would form a sort of marker between each layer of ice."

"Oh," said Miss Pickerell, beginning to understand. "The core that you would pull out of the hole in the ice would have these marks."

"Yes," the man said. "And if there was a lot of ice between two marks, we would know it had been a severe winter. If there was very little ice, that would indicate that the weather for that particular year had been very mild."

Miss Pickerell was fascinated. "It's a little like studying what the climate has been like by looking at the rings of a tree that has been sawed down, isn't it?"

"Very much like it," the man said. "But our equipment was hopelessly damaged when our plane came down."

All this time Foster had been up with the pilot and the co-pilot, and he stayed there while the co-pilot came back to say something to Miss Pickerell.

"I've been thinking about those pictures you took," he said. "I'm something of an amateur photographer and I could develop them for you as soon as we get to the air base if you'd let me. I'm very curious to see what they're like."

So, when the plane finally landed at the air base, and the official reports had been made, the co-pilot took Rosemary's camera from Miss Pickerell and disappeared.

The injured man had been taken to the air base's hospital, Foster was renewing acquaintances with some of his arctic friends, and Miss Pickerell was waiting in the communications center to ask somebody if it would be possible to talk to Dwight and Rosemary on their short-wave radio set. The two men from the weather expedition were already sending in a radio report to the scientific organization that had sponsored them. It wasn't a very cheerful report they were making.

The co-pilot came in the door with several large glossy pictures in his hand. He let in a blast of cold air and someone shouted, ''Shut that door!''

''You got some wonderful pictures, Miss Pickerell,'' the co-pilot said. ''Gives you a feeling of being right there. I made extra ones for myself. Hope you don't mind.''

''Of course not,'' Miss Pickerell said. ''I see you enlarged them.''

''Say, let me see those,'' one of the weather-expedition men said. He got up and took them from the co-pilot's hand, just as he was handing them to Miss Pickerell. He looked at them intently for a moment, and then rushed across to his companion who was just finishing his gloomy report about their failure.

"Hey, don't stop talking," the first man said. "Tell them we've made a mistake. Tell them we've been successful after all. Tell them we've got a perfect picture of the layers of ice—not in a glacier, but in the ice cap."

Miss Pickerell looked over his shoulder.

It was true. All the way along the cracked-off surface of the ice cap ran horizontal dark-colored bands. The fact that the picture had been enlarged made them especially clear.

"We never would have had this valuable information," the man said to Miss Pickerell, "if you hadn't taken these pictures."

"I never would have been *able* to take them," Miss Pickerell said, "if my niece Rosemary hadn't included her camera when she was packing for me."

They all hurried outside just then, because the first of the other rescue planes had arrived. All but Miss Pickerell—and the communications officer, who slammed his hand down angrily on the desk that held his communications equipment.

"This has got to stop!" he said. "All

afternoon somebody has been trying to get me to take a message. I suppose somebody thinks they're being very funny trying to give me a message about somebody's cow. No!" he shouted into his mouthpiece. "No, I *won't* take the message."

"Oh, please!" Miss Pickerell said, rushing toward him. "It's for me. It's from my niece and nephew. Can I talk to them?"

When he found out what it was all about the communications officer was quite helpful. "Their set isn't powerful enough to contact us directly, but there's another amateur operator in between who is relaying their messages. I'll let you talk to him."

17

Farewell to the Arctic

Miss Pickerell was really sorry when the time came for her to leave the air base and return home. She and Mr. Busby both had passage on a transpolar airliner that stopped there to refuel. In her short time there, she had learned to love the arctic.

But it would be good to get home to her cow, and to see Dwight and Rosemary again.

It was quite a pleasant surprise to find that Dwight and Rosemary were so interested in her experiences in the far north that they didn't turn on their short-wave radio set for a whole week. Not once did they tell her to "Sh!" They didn't even interrupt her, except to ask her questions.

The study of the layers of ice in the ice

cap showed a very definite pattern of severe winters and mild winters, for many years back. On the basis of this information it looked very much as if the coming winter would be very severe indeed.

The scientific organization that had sponsored the expedition announced that Miss Pickerell would be awarded a special citation because her photograph had been so important in making this prediction. But when Miss Pickerell insisted that Rosemary should have the credit, the organization announced there would be a double citation.

As soon as summer ended, on the very day, that Dwight and Rosemary returned to their own home, Miss Pickerell put her cow into the new winter trailer that Mr. Busby's factory had built especially for her cow, and traveled to the southern part of the country. After the rescue exploit, word of Model X24 had circulated around through the arctic, and Miss Pickerell had been urged to sell it there rather than to bring it home. Model X24 had proved itself in the arctic.

With Dwight and Rosemary helping her to study, Miss Pickerell had already been able to pass several examinations for licensed amateur radio operator—each more difficult than the last. She made many interesting unseen friends that winter by talking to them over the winter trailer's short-wave radio set.

Winter ended; Miss Pickerell and her cow returned home; Dwight and Rosemary came again to spend the summer; and it was now time to go to receive the citation from the scientific organization. When Rosemary's citation was presented, she made a very graceful short speech of thanks and both Miss Pickerell and Dwight were very proud of her. They all made the trip to the ceremony on the same train that Mr. Esticott was the conductor on.

Mr. Esticott was now reading the dictionary through, and he had got as far as *Te*.

"If you'd ever like to look up a word, Miss Pickerell," he said, "don't hesitate to let me know. And when I've got all the way through it—which will be sometime this summer—I'm going to give you this dictionary. Because you were so nice to me, Miss Pickerell, about letting me read your encyclopedia."

"Well, thank you," said Miss Pickerell. "But I won't be here this summer."

"You won't?"

"I got a short-wave radio message from Foster Esticott yesterday," Miss Pickerell said, and she smiled because the message had made her so happy. "Foster invited me to come to the arctic this summer. And I'm going. I'm going back again to the beautiful arctic regions."

ABOUT THE AUTHOR
AND ILLUSTRATOR

ELLEN MACGREGOR was born in Baltimore, Maryland, but moved to the West Coast and attended school in Washington. She received a degree in library sciences from the University of Washington. Her work in the library field has taken her all over the United States.

Ellen MacGregor created Miss Pickerell in the early 1950s and wrote four stories about her, as well as boxes of notes for future adventures. She died in 1954. Ten years later Miss Pickerell found Dora Pantell, who continued the series. The *Miss Pickerell* books are available in Archway Paperback editions.

PAUL GALDONE came to this country from Budapest, Hungary, and studied at the Art Students League in New York. He is a free-lance illustrator with many books to his credit. When Mr. Galdone is not working, he engages in his favorite pastime —being outdoors. He lives with his wife and two young children in Rockland County, New York.